CROSSWINDS PRESS, INC.
P.O. Box 683
Mystic, Connecticut 06355
crosswindspress.com

© 2011 by Crosswinds Press, Inc.

Printed in the United States of America

ISBN-139780982555996

10 9 8 7 6 5 4 3 2 1

Book design by Trish Sinsigalli LaPointe, LaPointe Design.
Old Mystic, Connecticut
tslapointedesign.com

Vive La Différance

BY CJ CONNOLLY
ILLUSTRATED BY LISA ADAMS

CROSSWINDS PRESS, INC.

To Aunt Cora, who could always
find a bit of sunshine in every person.

Prologue

This book is a continuation of the series that began with *Wil, Fitz and a Flea Named "T."* Mr. T is a wise old flea that has decided to help Wil learn a few of life's lessons while having fun along the way.

In this book, Mr. T avoids an invasion of a French Foreign Fleagion of fleas, much to Fitz's delight. He also helps Wil understand that it is the differences in people that make life fun. Instead of wanting everyone to be just like him, Wil ends up humming "Vive la Différance!"

The sun was shining, the sky oh so blue,
As Wil looked around for something to do.
Family day at the park, there were kids everywhere…
In fact he had cousins there, there and there!

Matthew was making castles in the sand,
While Grace and Ryan had swinging planned.
And Danny climbed high on the jungle gym,
Leaving only Wil alone, watching him.

"Danny, let's play hide and seek," Wil then said.
But Danny said "no" with a shake of his head.
Then Wil muttered softly, "Why can't he be…
Willing to play…to be just like me?"

Just as Wil was ready to give up on the fun,
He spotted the Other William on the run.
Beside him trotted his grey poodle Jacques,
Who carefully stepped around the rocks.

"Wil, want to play?" asked the Other William then.
It was play day it seemed all over again!
As the two boys ran off to play hide and seek,
Out of Jacques' fur a fleagion of fleas did peek!

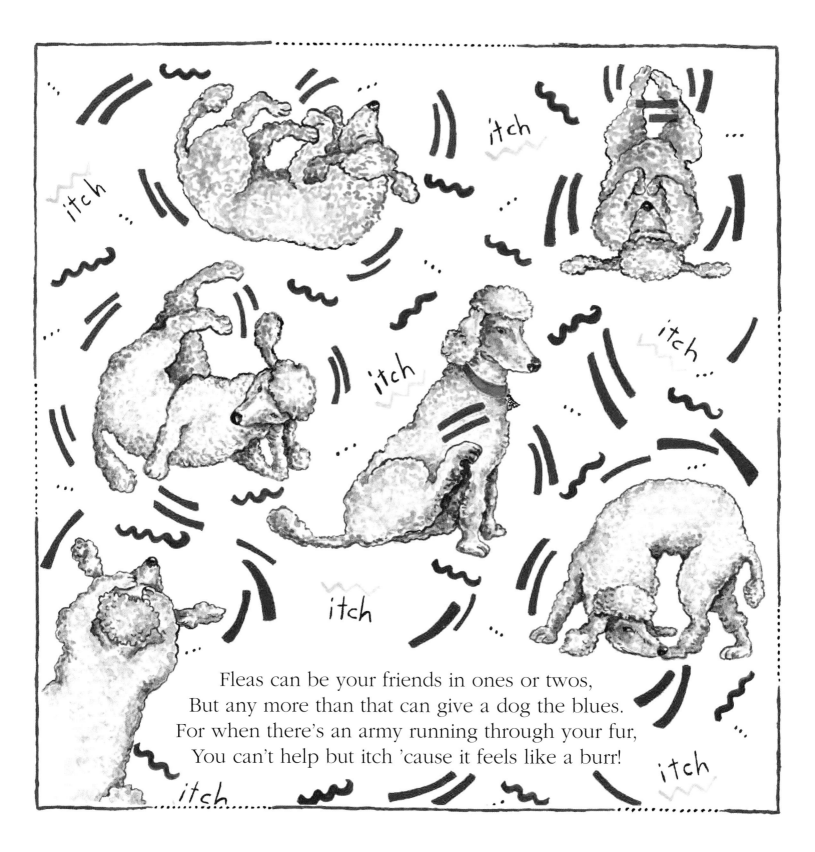

Fleas can be your friends in ones or twos,
But any more than that can give a dog the blues.
For when there's an army running through your fur,
You can't help but itch 'cause it feels like a burr!

Spotting trouble if this pack made for Fitz,
T drew himself up and said, "This ain't the Ritz!
I'd prefer if you'd stay on Jacques if you please.
Sorry fellas, this dog's taken, he belongs to me!"

Then T heard Fitz sigh, a small smile on his face,
For to be covered with fleas would be a disgrace.
Fitz was fond of T and the lessons he taught,
Yes, Mr. T was his friend, he liked him a lot.

Then both T and Fitz glanced over at Jacques,
As the fleas began to muster, there were a lot!
T knew that a fleagion would contain many more…
Oh no! There really were one hundred forty-four!

The Major General of Jacques' fleagion of fleas,
Saluted T and then turned in the breeze.
He called to his troops—a French Foreign Fleagion!
They'd been sent from France to scout out the region!

"Attention, I say, attention right now!"
Shouted Oui One, as he spoke to the crowd.
He got them in order, Oui Two, Three and Four,
Oui Ten, Oui Twenty, Oui Thirty and more!

Just as the troops were getting in line,
Oui One turned around to give them a sign.
As he stood at attention upon Jacques' shiny black nose,
He took one step backward…then in the air he froze!

T watched in shock as to the ground Oui One fell,
Then the troop of French fleas moved forward as well!
It seemed they were following, just part of a pack,
That was walking right off of the nose of old Jacques!

"Sacré Bleu!" Oui One did then say,
As flat upon the ground he lay.
He didn't have time to say much more,
As right beside him fell Oui Two, Three and Four!

Then "splat, splat, splat" Oui One did hear,
As one by one his fleagion fell near.
It was an awful sight, it made him quite queasy,
For the fleas were all falling way too easy!

With a shake of his head and a modest sigh,
Oui One then got to his feet as gurneys flew by.
He limped to the hospital set up in the grass,
That was filled with flea doctors, both lads and lass.

T smiled a bit when he spotted old Oui Eight.
He'd stepped out of line, remaining on Jacques' pate.
Neither could believe the sight down below.
The fleas tried to rise, but some were really quite slow.

"I cannot believe what I see," said Oui Eight.
"Did they not think about their bleak fate?
They marched forward with nary a thought,
As if doing battle, but they never fought!"

"I agree with you, Oui Eight," T did say,
"It has truly been an unusual day.
For I have never seen a fleagion of fleas,
Simply walk off a cliff," noted Mr. T.

T and Oui Eight then looked down in surprise,
As Oui One grabbed his crutches with pride in his eyes.
Behind him fell in Oui Two, Three and Four.
The French Foreign fleas were marching once more!

They fell into line, with crutches and slings,
For broken legs and other bruised things.
And they moved forward bravely behind old Oui One.
A new flea campaign had clearly begun!

Up Jacques' leg they marched as he looked on in chagrin.
T simply hoped they wouldn't do it all over again!
Then T turned his attention back to young Wil,
Who waved as the Other William went over the hill.

"Wil, what are you going to do now?" asked Mr. T.
"As your friend had to go with his family?
Are you going to swing or play in the sand?
What's on your mind, what is your plan?"

"I don't know, T," Wil said slightly sadly.
"I'd like to play tag, I'd like to run badly!
But it seems everyone has other things to do,
Leaving me feeling kind of blue!"

T thought for a moment, then quickly told,
Wil about the French fleas who had been very bold.
Following their leader, though, had not been too bright.
It seemed fairly crazy, clearly not at all right!

"What do you think, Wil, as you ponder the story,
Which hopefully I haven't made too gory.
Did it make sense to follow or to step out of line?
For when I left him, Oui Eight was doing just fine!"

"Life would be boring if we were all the same,
Even if everyone else would agree to our games.
Variety is the spice of life," said wise Mr. T.
"It's what makes life fun for you and for me."

It dawned on Wil then what Mr. T was saying,
As all around him his family was playing.
It was how they were different that made life fun.
"Vive la Différance!" he began to hum.

As Wil looked on, then what did he see?
That everyone was just the way they should be!
"I'll celebrate the differences, though crazy it seems!"
Said Wil to his friend, his voice full of glee!

So Wil settled back and watched with a smile,
As Grace and Ryan went sliding a while.
And Matthew continued to play in the sand.
With Danny beside him, one big happy band.

Note: The author has taken poetic license in spelling Différence with an "a", i.e., Différance, to enhance the rhyming.